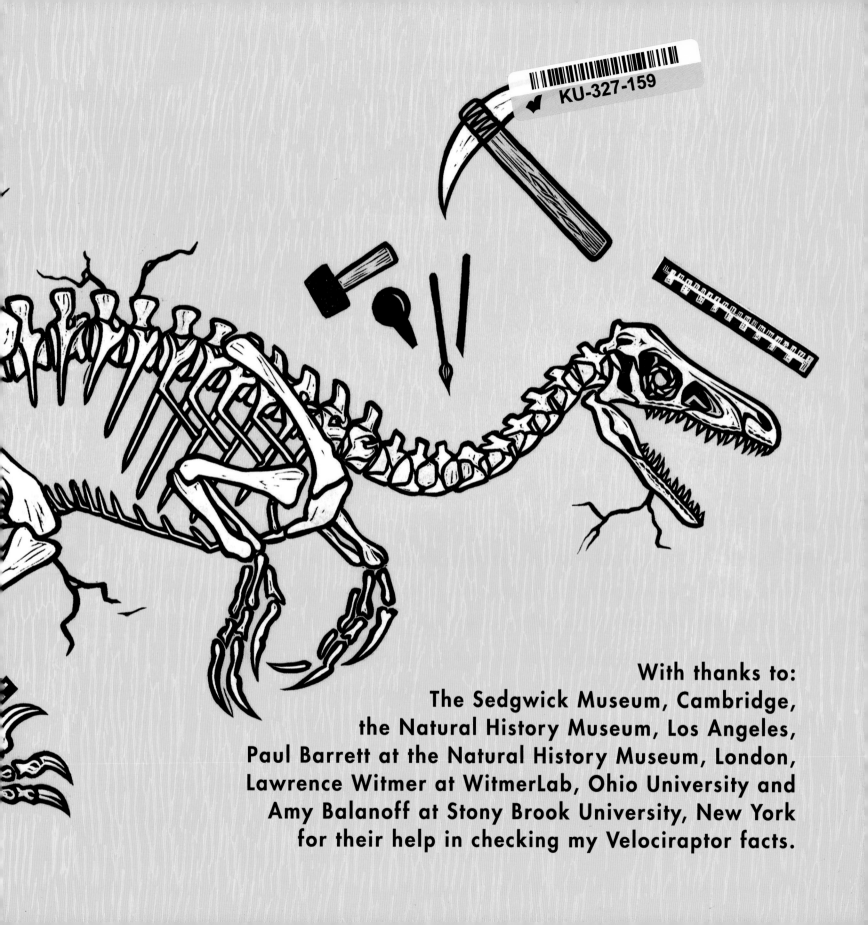

With thanks to:
The Sedgwick Museum, Cambridge,
the Natural History Museum, Los Angeles,
Paul Barrett at the Natural History Museum, London,
Lawrence Witmer at WitmerLab, Ohio University and
Amy Balanoff at Stony Brook University, New York
for their help in checking my Velociraptor facts.

To my brother, Rick, for being my partner in crime … A.L.

First published in Great Britain in 2021 by Boxer Books Limited.
This paperback edition published in Great Britain in 2022.

Boxer® is a registered trademark of Boxer Books Limited.

www.boxerbooks.com

Text and illustrations copyright © 2021 Alison Limentani
The right of Alison Limentani to be identified as the author and illustrator
of this work has been asserted by her in accordance with the Copyright,
Designs and Patents Act, 1988.

The illustrations were prepared using lino cuts and
collagraphs and digital editing. The text is set in Futura.

ISBN 978-1-914912-06-1

1 3 5 7 9 10 8 6 4 2

Printed in China

All of our papers are sourced
from managed forests and
renewable resources.

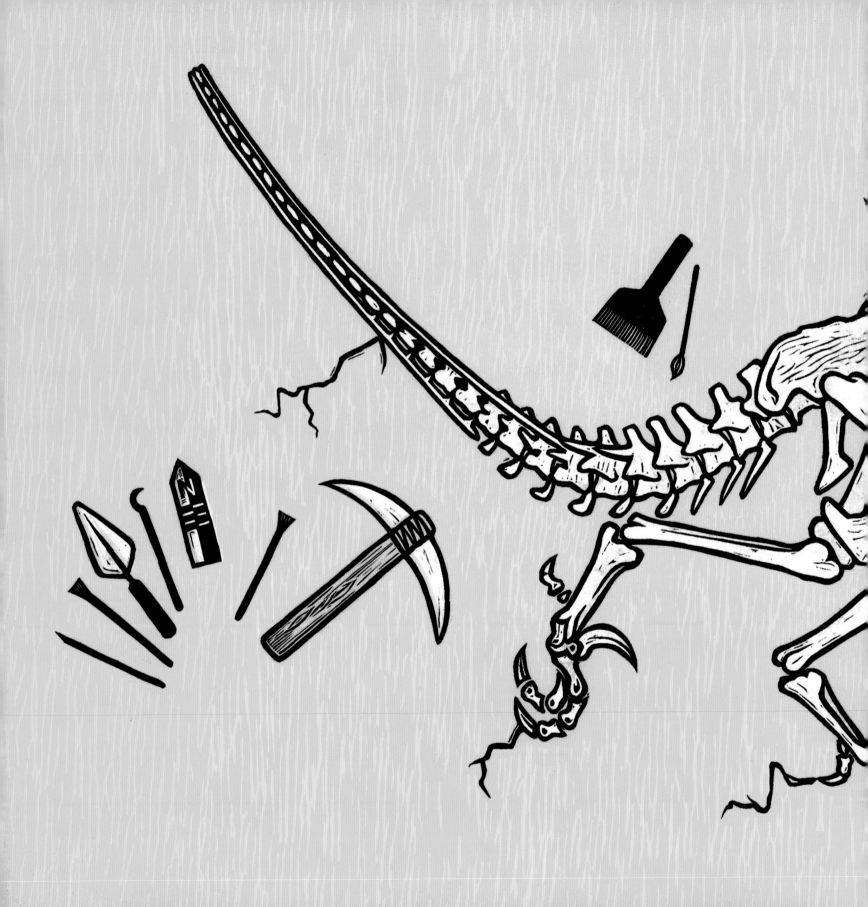

HOW FAST WAS A VELOCIRAPTOR?

ALISON LIMENTANI

Boxer Books

Velociraptors are believed to be one of the fastest dinosaurs, but what do we really know about them?

Scientists think they were feathered like birds.

But they could not fly.

People imagine that all dinosaurs were enormous. Actually a Velociraptor was only as big as a turkey.

Though it was much more fierce!

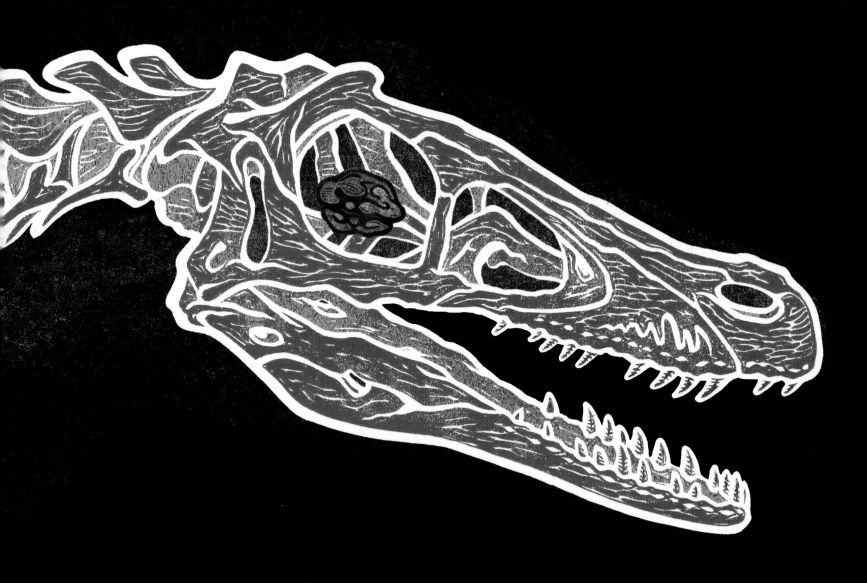

Velociraptors had a relatively large brain for their size. This means they were probably quite clever.

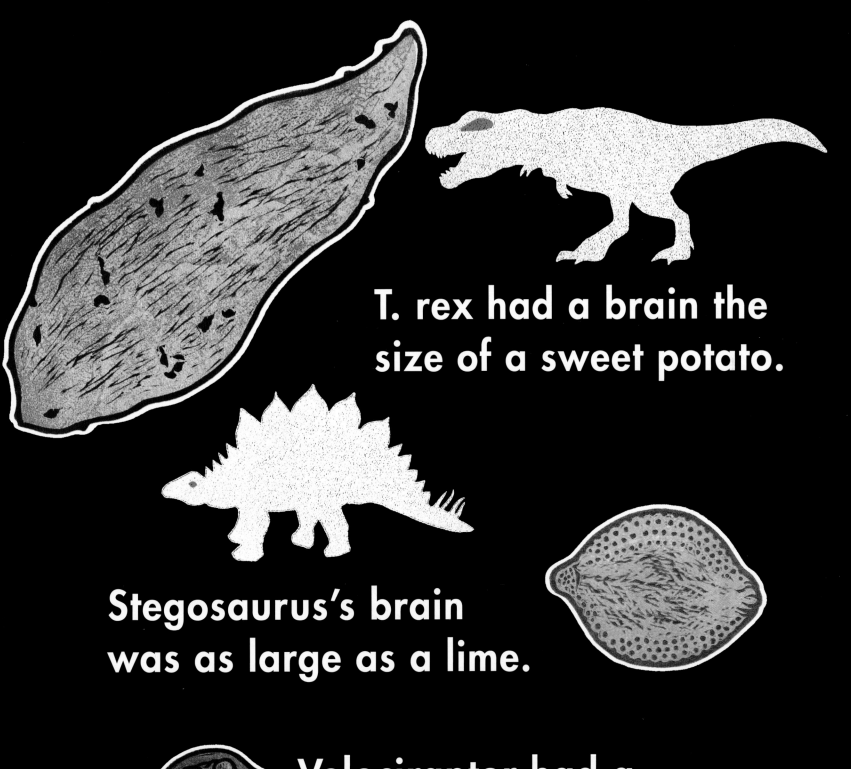

T. rex had a brain the size of a sweet potato.

Stegosaurus's brain was as large as a lime.

Velociraptor had a walnut-sized brain.
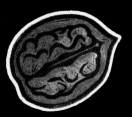

Velociraptors were meat-eaters. They had sharp teeth and claws to help them catch their prey.

They could see in the dark so they could sneak up on their dinner!

But how fast was a Velociraptor?

Scientists usually work this out by measuring the distance between the footprints of fossilised dinosaur tracks.

Unfortunately no Velociraptor tracks have been found yet.

Until tracks are found, scientists try to work out Velociraptor speed using computers...

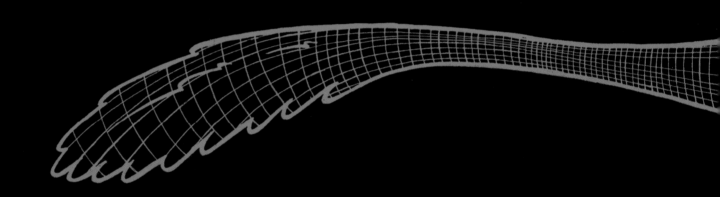

Weight = 12.5 kilos
Height = up to 50cm at the hips
Length = 2m head to tail

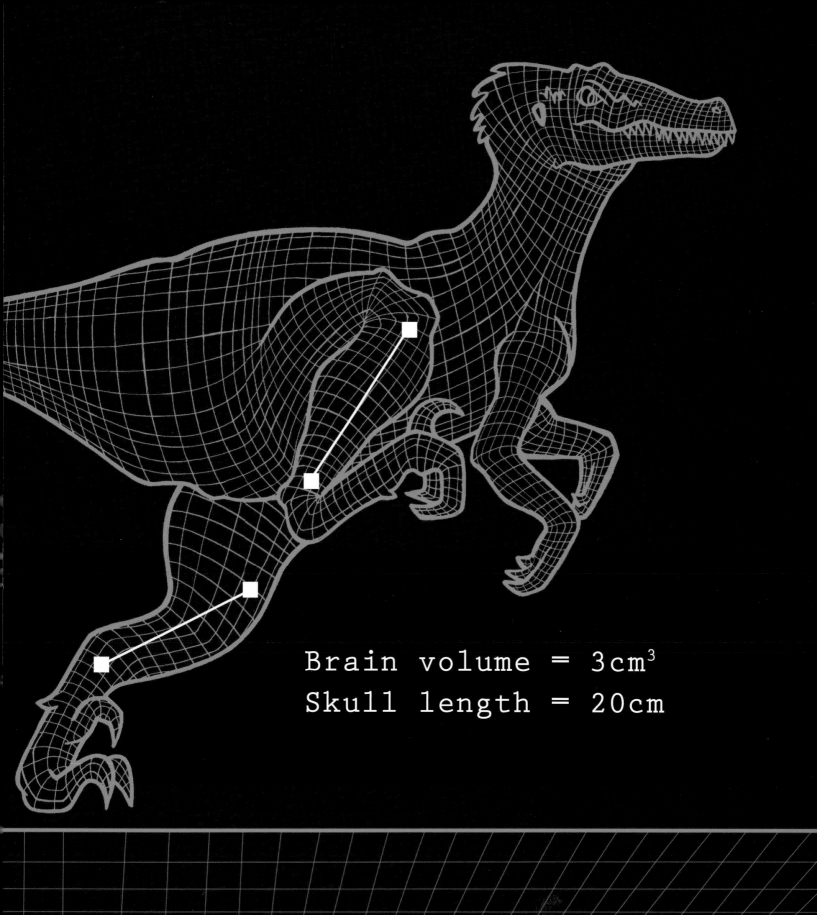

Brain volume = 3cm³
Skull length = 20cm

Or by building robots based on fossils and living animals.

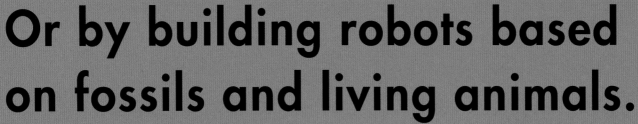
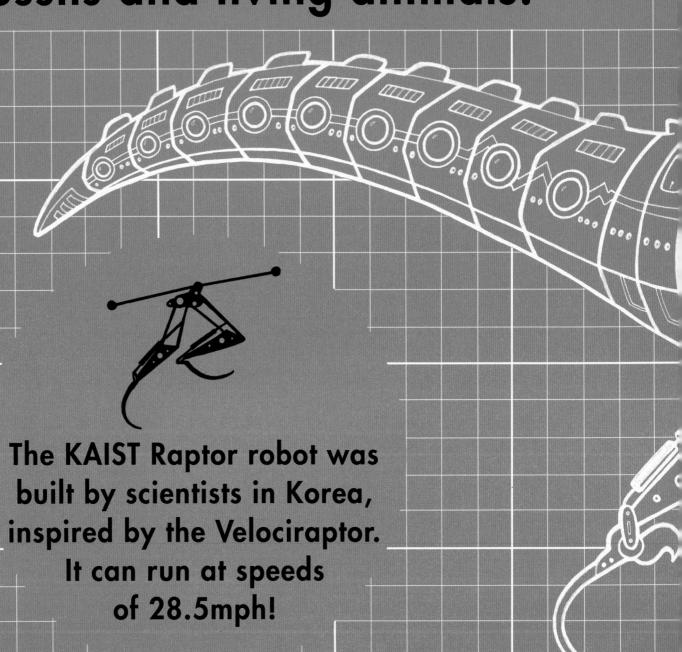

The KAIST Raptor robot was
built by scientists in Korea,
inspired by the Velociraptor.
It can run at speeds
of 28.5mph!

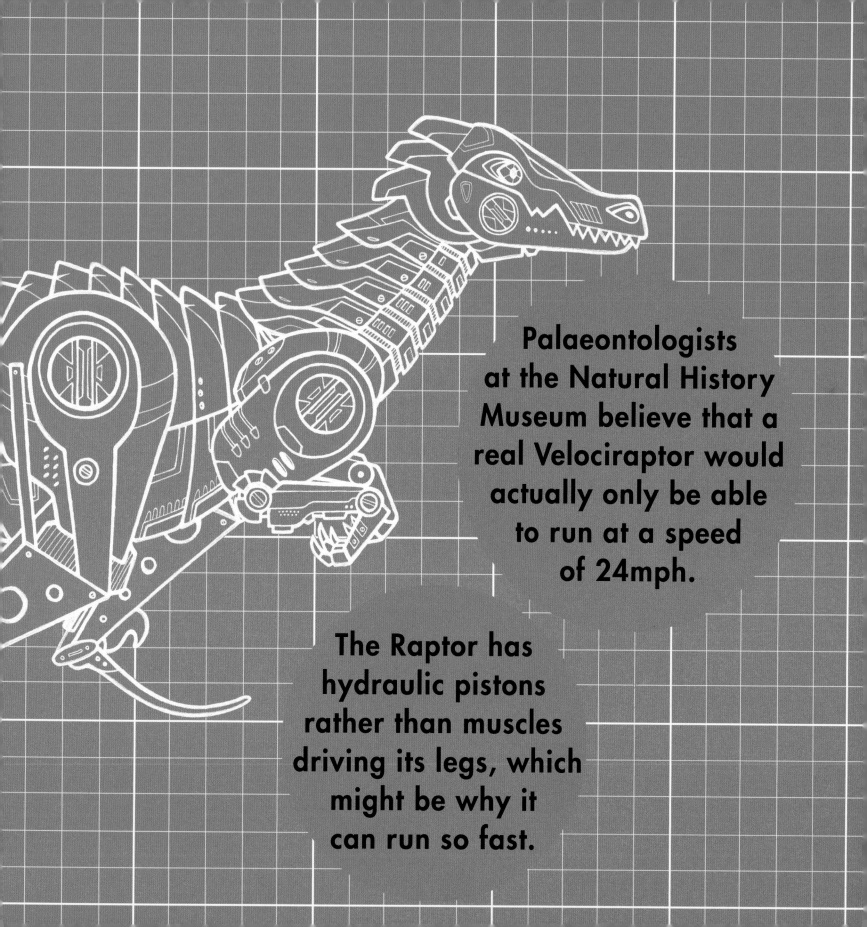

Palaeontologists at the Natural History Museum believe that a real Velociraptor would actually only be able to run at a speed of 24mph.

The Raptor has hydraulic pistons rather than muscles driving its legs, which might be why it can run so fast.

We think a Velociraptor could have run faster than . . .

2mph
(walking)
22mph
(swimming)

0.03mph

8mph

a snail,   a penguin,   a mouse

11mph

24mph

and a pig.

This means a Velociraptor could run faster than . . .

5mph

3mph

you can run,   kayak

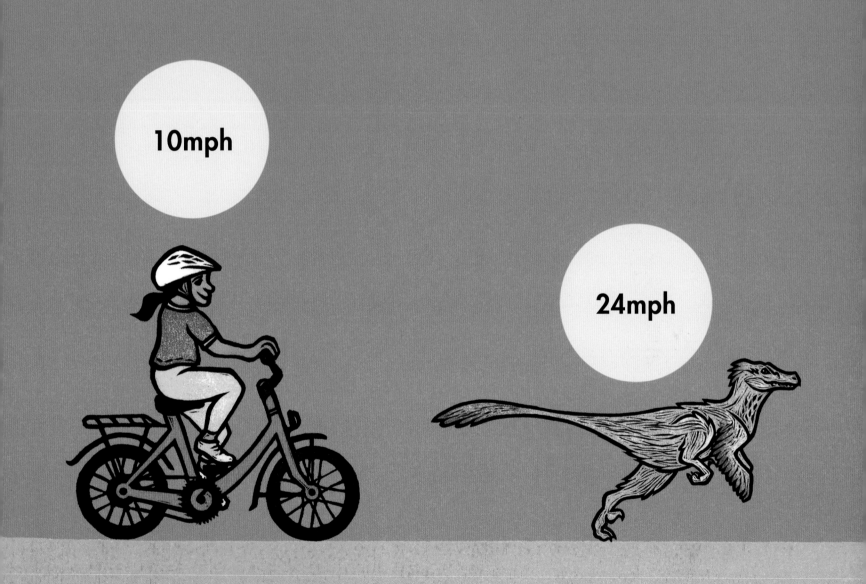

or even cycle!

This is quite fast, but it is still not as fast as . . .

24mph

30mph

45mph

a cat,   an ostrich,

242mph

a peregrine falcon,

50mph

70mph

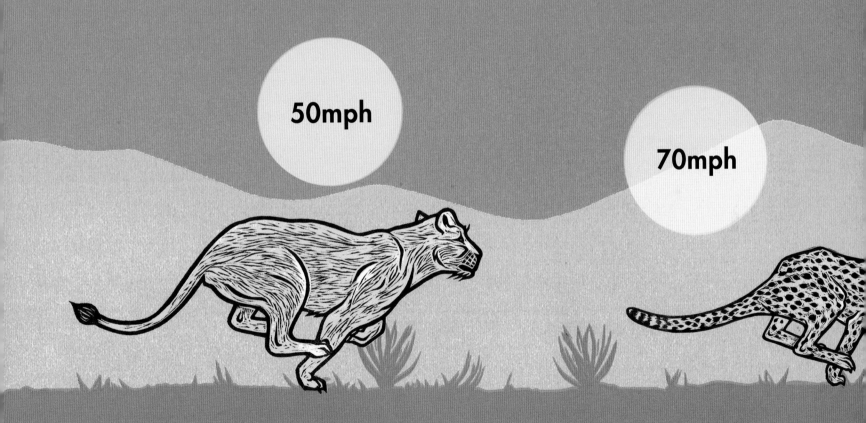

a lion,   or a cheetah.

And slower than . . .

30mph

24mph

a bus

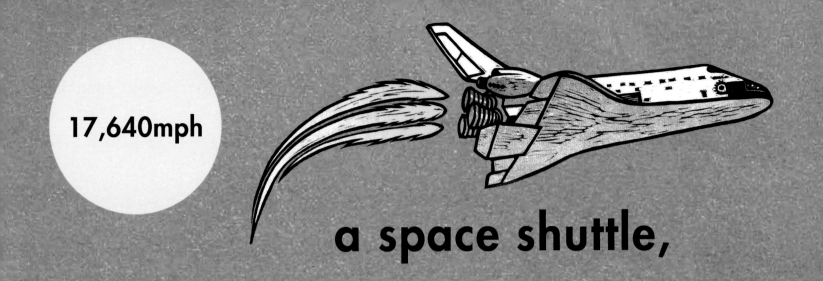

17,640mph

a space shuttle,

200mph

and a racing car.

We will never
know for sure,

but a Velociraptor was probably as fast as . . .

a turkey!

70mph

200mph

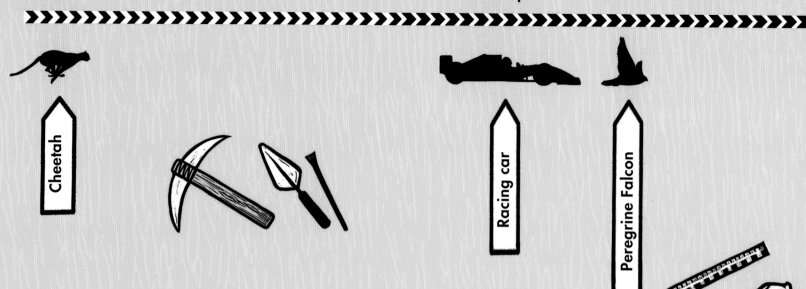

Cheetah

Racing car

Peregrine Falcon

Scientists can learn a lot about dinosaurs by looking at fossils and comparing them to modern-day animals. The facts in this book are based on the latest Velociraptor findings. We may never find out how fast a Velociraptor was, but who knows what else we might discover in the future!

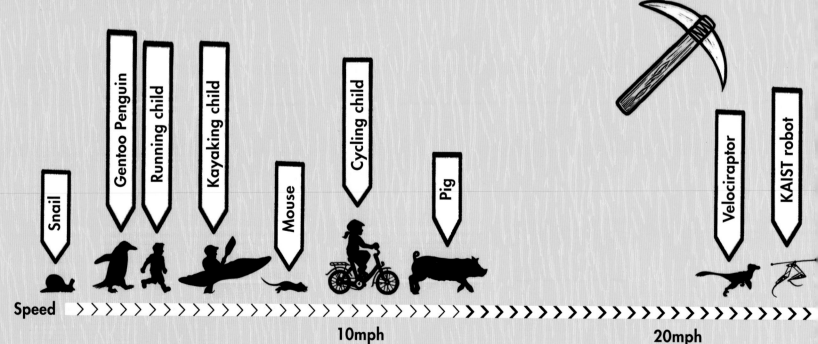

Snail

Gentoo Penguin

Running child

Kayaking child

Mouse

Cycling child

Pig

Velociraptor

KAIST robot

Speed

10mph

20mph

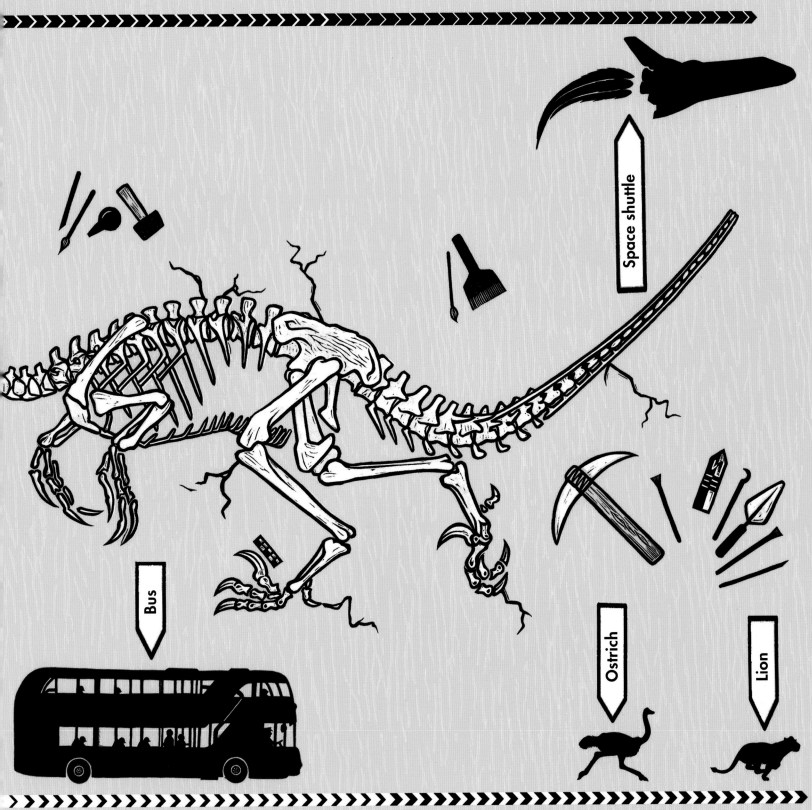

17,640mph

Space shutle

Bus

Ostrich

Lion

30mph

40mph

50mph